Give Me Grace

A Child's Daybook of Prayers

Cynthia Rylant

Simon & Schuster Books for Young Readers

Simon & Schuster Books for Young Readers
An Imprint of Simon & Schuster Children's Publishing Division
1230 Avenue of the Americas, New York, New York 10020

Book design by Anahid Hamparian
The text for this book is set in Dana.
The paintings in this book were done using acrylics.

Printed in the United States of America
10 9 8 7 6 5 4 3 2 1

Library of Congress Cataloging-in-Publication Data

Rylant, Cynthia.
Give me grace : a child's daybook of prayers / Cynthia Rylant.—1st ed.
p.   cm.
Summary: Presents seven prayers in rhyme, one for each day of the week.
ISBN 0-689-82293-6
1. Children—Prayer-books and devotions—English. [1. Prayer books
and devotions.] I. Title.
BL625.5.R954   1999
291.4'33—dc21
98-49368

For Kevin

Monday make me
good and kind
to all creatures
that I find.
Help me love God's
whole creation.
Make my life a
celebration.

Tuesday

Tuesday teach me
faith and caring,
teach me wisdom,
teach me sharing.
Raise me up and
make me strong.
Be with me
the whole day long.

Wednesday make me
full of light.
Guide my heart both
day and night.
Give me gladness,
give me grace.
Shine your love
upon my face.

Thursday open up
my eyes
to your angels in
the skies.
Let me know their
wings are near me,
and that they will
always hear me.

Friday

Friday keep the
ones I love.
Comfort them from
up above.
Lift their hearts
and hold them dear.
Help them know that
you are here.

Saturday in
early morn
make me thankful
I was born.
Give my spirit
peace within.
Let each day
with hope begin.

Sunday in

a quiet time,

bless this little

life of mine.

In the wonder of

each day,

let me live

a holy way.

Amen